# Demi's Adventures

# What's in the Kitchen

Written by Shanice D. Oliver
Illustrated by Kayla R. Dowdy

## THE SEED SOWERS CLUB:
### Dedicated to education young children of color

Amanda Collier
Britney Holmes
Chiquita Bonds
Cicero & Sammiestein Hall
Darry & Cynthia Dowdy
Darry Dowdy Jr.
Debra Hall
Elicia Spearman
Erica Goss
Ivan Oliver Sr.
Ivan Oliver Jr.
Jane Venson-Talford
Josephine Franklin
Judy C Martin
Kinsey Moritz
Kristopher Brewer
Ladarrius Griffin
Martha Perine Beard
Ronald Patrick
Stephen Kirnon
Tavaris Boga
The Lavish By Lauren, LLC

ISBN 979-8-5455-3783-9
www.flawlessdesigns.org

Demi loves taking summer visits
to Grandma Virginia's house.

We Prayed

We laughed

We Played

They laugh, play and even go to church to pray.

On the car ride home, Grandma Virginia asked, "What's for dinner?" Demi did not have a clue what she wanted and asked Grandma Virginia, "What's in the kitchen?"

They made it home, took a look  and
found so many foods!

# Meat

Sausage  Shrimp

# Vegetables

Bell pepper  Garlic  Okra

Onion  Celery

Demi found shrimp and sausage, onions, okra, celery, garlic and bell peppers.
Mmmmm... mmmm... mmmm...

Grandma Virginia found a  box of brown rice
and the perfect seasonings,  with  the chicken
broth pot.
Mmmmm... mmmm... mmmm...

Grandma Virginia is cooking in the kitchen!

It's gumbo in Grandma
Virginia's kitchen.

# Gumbo

- ○ Shrimp
- ○ Sausage
- ○ Onions
- ○ Okra
- ○ Celery
- ○ garlic
- ○ bell peppers
- ○ Brown rice
- ○ Chicken broth
- ○ Seasonings

# Author: Shanice D. Oliver

Shanice D. Oliver is an author, mother, entrepreneur and philanthropist from Memphis, TN with the passion to create unique family learning experiences to foster growth and empathy. For over 20 years, she has served many local, national and global communities to ensure they are equipped with technology, food, and other essentials to nourish the family unit. Shanice has excelled as a student athlete from elementary to high school, and has graduated with honors and prestigious recognition from Christian Brother's University'15 and Pepperdine University'18.

Shanice enjoys working with technology, visiting museums and playing with her family, dogs & friends. She is also an active member of Alpha Kappa Alpha Sorority, Inc., Junior League of Memphis and mentor young professionals across the U.S.

# Illustrator: Kayla R. Dowdy

Kayla Dowdy is an 14 year old artist and entrepreneur from Memphis, TN. She started her art journey at Germanshire Elementary under the watchful eye of Mrs. Pigues. Kayla later was accepted to the Colonial Middle School Capa Art program through the encouragement of Ms. Webb and the direction of Mrs. Shiberou. Kayla credits her professional work ethics to her dancer instructor Ms. Chauniece Thompson with Ballet on Wheels. Kayla's art has been displayed at Stax Museum and Memphis Rocks in Memphis Tn. Kayla has won several awards and received honorable mention for her art.

Kayla enjoys sewing and creating unique designs in her spare time when she is not spending time with her family and friends. Kayla is a member of Girls and Pearls at Colonial Middle School and has received numerous academic honors.

# DEMI'S ADVENTURES BOOK SERIES

Demi's Adventures:
The Hopscotch Calendar Game

Demi's Adventures:
What's In The Kitchen

Demi's Adventures:
International Pet Festival

Made in the USA
Columbia, SC
13 October 2024

44179742R00015